GREAT GREEN GATOR GRADUATION

Want more books by Debbie Dadey?

Swamp Monster in Third Grade

Swamp Monster in Third Grade #2:
Lizards in the Lunch Line

Swamp Monster in Third Grade #3:
Trapped in the Principal's Office

The Slime Wars

Slime Time!

And don't forget to check out . . .

Ghostville Elementary®

BY DEBBIE DADEY AND MARCIA THORNTON JONES

GREAT GREEN GATOR GRADUATION

BY DEBBIE DADEY
ILLUSTRATIONS BY MARGEAUX LUCAS

A
LITTLE APPLE
PAPERBACK

SCHOLASTIC INC.
NEW YORK TORONTO LONDON AUCKLAND SYDNEY
MEXICO CITY NEW DELHI HONG KONG BUENOS AIRES

To Lauren McGuinty, who suggested the title, and Amelia Schwartz, our junior editor

ISBN 0-439-79401-3

12 11 10 9 8 7 6 5 4 3 2 6 7 8 9 10 11/0

Printed in the U.S.A. 40
First printing, May 2006

CONTENTS

1

The Big One

"It's The Big One!" Nancy yelled to her brother. They stared at each other with yellow swamp-monster eyes, their green skin bright with fear. They were in the swamp, hidden underneath the roots of a huge mangrove tree, collecting flies for their dad's famous pudding.

Jake gasped as a huge alligator crawled out of the swamp and crept in the tall grass toward a girl sitting on a brightly painted park bench. He knew that webless creature!

He also knew that gator. Being a swamp monster, Jake knew every local alligator by name. The Big One was the oldest and largest alligator ever to slither through a swamp. He weighed more than six hundred pounds and was at least nineteen feet long. Usually alligators were friendly enough to swamp monsters, but not this one. Even the best gator wrestlers steered clear of The Big One because he was so mean and deadly.

"Emily!" Jake shouted, the green points of his hair popping out of the swamp. "Look out!" Why didn't anyone help her? There were hundreds of school kids sitting on bleachers in front of a recently built stage. Emily's bench was just behind the crowd. But all of the people had their eyes on the woman on the stage. Jake knew that woman was the school principal, Mrs. Pellman. Why didn't the principal stop the alligator? Instead, the woman talked about behaving at the upcoming graduation ceremony.

Why did she care about how kids acted, when someone was about to get eaten?

"I'll go for help," Nancy said, disappearing under the murky water. Jake's sister could swim faster than any other swamp monster in his family, but Jake worried she wouldn't be fast enough.

"No!" Jake yelled as The Big One started to snap at Emily's shoe.

The Big One closed his mouth in surprise. Then he hissed again, and his huge teeth glistened in the afternoon sun. Jake knew what was coming. The Big One was going to have Emily for an afternoon snack.

Jake didn't think about how dangerous it was for a swamp monster to be out of the swamp in broad daylight, or how he'd promised his parents not to visit his friend Emily again. Jake didn't think at all. He

jumped out of the water and threw himself toward The Big One.

Emily screamed as The Big One and the swamp monster rolled on the ground by her feet. Dust flew everywhere, and huge jaws snapped at her and at Jake.

Emily's screams brought people running. "Someone is wrestling an alligator," shouted a teacher.

"That's the biggest alligator I've ever seen!" called a kid beside her.

"Somebody do something!" Emily yelled. "Call the police! Call the fire department! Call the army!" Kids screamed and cried along with their teachers.

Suddenly all the snapping and yelling stopped. Everything was quiet. Deadly quiet.

2

Caught

"Jake!" Emily screamed. Jake didn't answer. In fact, no one made a sound. About ten brave people crowded closer to the alligator, including Emily's good friend Tommy.

"I think the alligator's knocked out," one of the adults whispered.

"Who did it?" asked a skinny kid named Ryan.

"Jake," whimpered Emily. "He saved my life. He must be trapped under the alligator."

"Jake is a hero," Tommy said. "We have

to get him out of there." Tommy and Emily tugged on The Big One's tail.

"What if that gator wakes up?" a teacher said. "He could eat us all. Everyone get back."

"You mean there's a kid under that alligator?" Principal Pellman asked.

Emily, Tommy, Ryan, Principal Pellman, and several strong teachers lifted the alligator's tail. They saw a very still green body underneath. Suddenly, they heard groaning. "It's Jake," Emily said. "He's alive!"

It took all of Emily's and Tommy's strength, but they managed to pull Jake out from under the gator.

"Let's get him away from that alligator," suggested a first-grade teacher, "just in case it wakes up."

One of the teachers carried Jake away

from the swamp and onto a concrete sidewalk. "What's wrong with him?" whispered a fourth-grader. "He's green and his head is pointed."

Another kid shrugged. "Maybe the alligator threw up on him or something."

Emily and Tommy didn't tell the crowd, but they knew that Jake's skin was normally green and that his hair always stood

up in dark green spikes. After all, Jake was a swamp monster and their friend.

"Look," Ryan said. "He's waking up."

Jake sat up and rubbed his eyes. His head felt like it had been smashed with a rock. His body ached and his skin felt cold and tingly. What had happened? Why was he out of the swamp?

Jake opened his eyes and was confused for a moment. He was surrounded by webless creatures! Some of them were full grown, and they were reaching for him. He was trapped!

"Look at his yellow eyes," whispered the music teacher. "The poor boy."

Another kid came up behind the crowd and peered over everyone's shoulders. "That's no boy. That's a swamp monster!"

3

Dead

"No, he's not a swamp monster," Emily said, with her fingers crossed behind her back. "That's just a costume."

"Why is he wearing a costume?" a fifth-grade girl asked. "It's not Halloween yet."

"It doesn't matter," Emily said, patting Jake on his pointy head. "He saved my life."

"Good job," Principal Pellman told Jake. "You truly are a hero. In fact, you just inspired me. You should give a speech at the sixth-grade graduation ceremony next week. We can call it 'Words from a Hero.'"

Jake opened his mouth, but he was so

weak that nothing would come out. He wanted to tell them he couldn't stay on dry land for a week. Swamp monsters weren't made to be out of water that long. Besides, nothing would scare him more than having to talk in front of a huge crowd, especially a crowd of humans.

"Jake would be delighted," Emily answered for him.

Principal Pellman smiled. "Then it's settled. We'd better get back to school. That's enough graduation practice for one day. Do you need help walking, Jake?"

Jake shook his head, even though his legs felt like swamp grass.

"But what about the alligator?" a young teacher asked. "Isn't it dangerous?"

Principal Pellman gave The Big One a soft kick in the side. "Looks dead to me."

As the classes trooped back to the school, Emily stayed behind. She touched Jake's shoulder. "Are you all right?" she asked.

Jake blushed. Emily always made him feel that way. "I'm fine. Did The Big One hurt you?" he asked.

"The Big One?" Emily asked.

Jake nodded at the enormous, silent alligator. "That's what we swamp monsters call that huge gator."

"He is big all right," Emily whispered. "How did you kill him?"

Jake shook his head. "I don't think I did. Maybe he was older that we thought and he died of old age."

"Thanks for saving me," Emily said with a shy smile.

Jake felt his green face turning red. "I won't be able to speak at the graduation. I have to get back to the swamp."

Emily hung her head, and her dark hair hid her face. "I understand," she said.

Jake was so busy looking at Emily, he didn't notice that one of the gator's eyes had popped open. "It's just that I promised my parents I wouldn't mess around with humans again. It's pretty dangerous for a swamp monster."

Emily nodded. "I understand," she said again.

"Good-bye," Jake told Emily. He turned to go when suddenly a huge roar came from the alligator. "Run!" Jake yelled to Emily. "Catch up with your class!"

"I can't leave you here with that beast," Emily said.

"I'll be fine," Jake lied. He pushed Emily toward the sidewalk and dove into the swamp. The alligator slid into the water after Jake, with its mouth open wide.

4

Stone Casserole

"Jake!" Nancy yelled. "Over here!" Jake swam toward Nancy as fast as his webbed feet would carry him. Unfortunately, The Big One managed to swim just as fast. Jake had never seen an alligator move so quickly, but he'd never been chased by one before, either.

"Did you bring help?" Jake asked as he reached Nancy.

"I brought Mom and Dad. Everyone else was too scared to come." Jake could have kissed his parents, except there was a giant alligator lunging toward him.

Jake leaped out of the way just as his dad

brought his cooking pot down on The Big One's rounded snout. The Big One swayed for a moment, and Jake thought his dad had defeated the big gator in one swift move. But The Big One shook his head and lunged again, this time grabbing one handle of the pot in his mouth.

"Not my cooking pot!" Dad hollered, and he pulled with all his might. Jake knew how prized that pot was. After all, they lived in a swamp. Pots weren't easy to find.

Jake's mother jumped on The Big One's back and started singing. His mom's pretty voice had always put Jake to sleep when he was little, but would it work on the biggest alligator to ever hit the swamp?

The Big One hissed, but he kept his death grip on the cooking pot. Jake grabbed the other pot handle and pulled with his dad.

The Big One wasn't letting go. Then Nancy got an idea. She lifted the lid off the pot. The wonderful smell of stone-and-crawfish casserole drifted over the swamp.

The Big One's nostrils got bigger and bigger as he breathed in the delicious smell. "Give it to him," ordered Mom.

"But that's our supper," Jake's dad complained.

"Just do it," Mom said, jumping off the huge creature's back.

With a big sigh, Jake's dad heaved the casserole, with its stone topping, onto the gator's head. With a big snap, The Big One swallowed it all up. Then, with a satisfied look on his face, he slowly swam off toward the deepest part of the swamp. "Thank you for saving me," Jake told his family with a huge lump in his throat.

Nancy grinned. "Thank goodness Dad is such a great cook."

"And now, we need to talk about your punishment for going near humans again," Jake's dad said with a frown on his face.

5

A Promise

Swish. Swish. Nancy sloshed over to Jake's bedroom grotto, which was built out of the remains of an old van that someone had dumped deep in the swamp. Jake's door was closed, and Nancy opened it without knocking. The rusty door squeaked, and Jake quickly stuffed his collection of human clothing into the glove box and slammed it shut. If his parents saw what he'd hidden, they'd probably take it away. They frowned upon his interest in webless creatures.

"Haven't you ever heard of privacy?" Jake asked.

Nancy didn't say anything. She just plopped down on the weed-covered car seat and looked at her fins.

"What's wrong with you?" Jake asked. It wasn't like Nancy to be quiet. She never ran out of things to say.

Nancy looked at Jake but still didn't say anything. It made Jake nervous. He had a very bad feeling. Something horrible must have happened.

"What is it? What's going on?" Jake plopped down on the seat beside his sister.

Nancy slowly shook her head. "Nothing has happened."

Jake breathed a sigh of relief before Nancy added, "Yet."

Suddenly Jake was very cold. He grabbed a handful of mud from the floor of his bedroom and rubbed it over his arms. Mud was a good insulator for swamp monsters. The colder it got, the more mud they rubbed on. But Jake still felt chilled. Nancy knew something, and whatever it was must be really terrible.

"Just tell me," Jake said, rubbing more mud onto his legs.

"Remember last month when I helped Aunt Freda put swamp grass into jars?" Nancy said.

Jake nodded. Aunt Freda was the weirdest aunt anyone could ever hope to have. She kept all sorts of jars filled with strange jellied creatures and plants. She also had hundreds of scrolls lining the walls of her cave. Once, when Jake had tried to look at the writing on one of the scrolls, she had slapped his hand and told him they were secret. Jake tried to keep away from Aunt Freda, but Nancy liked her.

SWAMP THING

"Aunt Freda taught me to speak alligator," Nancy said.

Jake's mouth fell wide open. He had never heard of such a thing. His sister had a special way with animals, but no swamp monster could communicate with alligators. "Impossible," Jake said.

Nancy grabbed some mud and rubbed it on her arms. She used a small twig to comb the bugs out of her hair. Whenever she found a bug, she popped it in her mouth.

"Aunt Freda made me promise not to tell, but she knows the languages of many creatures, and she taught me alligator."

"Why are you telling me this?" Jake asked. Nancy didn't usually break promises.

"Because the alligator hissed something," Nancy said. "Something terrible."

Jake gulped and sat on the floor of the muddy van. He dug his webbed feet deep into the mud. He closed his eyes as Nancy told him the bad news.

"The Big One vowed to come back and eat Emily," Nancy whispered.

Jake jumped up and hit his head on the rusty van roof. "I have to warn Emily!" he shouted.

6

The Most Terrifying Monster

"You can't," Nancy told Jake. "You promised Mom and Dad that you wouldn't see Emily again."

Jake lowered his head. A swamp monster's promise meant something, and Jake would never break his word unless it was serious. "You promised Aunt Freda you wouldn't tell anyone about talking to alligators."

Nancy's yellow eyes closed. Jake knew she felt bad about not keeping her word. "I know, but I had to warn you," she whispered.

"And I have to warn Emily," Jake said. "A swamp monster never forgets a friend."

Nancy nodded. She knew Jake was right, but she didn't want him to risk going near The Big One again. Sure, Nancy had wrestled plenty of little alligators before, but The Big One was the most terrifying creature in the swamp. Nancy couldn't forget how he'd tried to eat Jake. "It's just so dangerous," Nancy told her brother.

"I'll be careful," Jake said. Jake knew what he had to do, but that night he had trouble sleeping. He tossed and turned and pounded his mud pillow, but every time he nodded off he dreamed of huge snapping jaws.

All the next morning, Jake watched the swamp from the safety of a big mangrove tree's roots. The sun beat down, and flies swarmed around his face. Occasionally a fly would land on his green cheek. He quickly caught it with his tongue for a snack. Jake began to hope that the students from Glenstone Elementary wouldn't be coming back to the swamp again. Maybe seeing the huge alligator yesterday would keep them away.

Unfortunately, just as Jake was leaning his head against a tree root for a nap, a long line of children was tromping through the bushes and filing onto the bleachers in front of their new stage. Principal Pellman stood on the stage and addressed the students: "We only have one more day to practice for the graduation ceremony. Let's start with the school song."

While the kids sang, "Glenstone School we love you so. In our hearts you'll always go . . . ," Jake crawled out of the swamp toward a girl in the back row. She had long black hair just like Emily.

His skin tingled in the air, even though it was warm. Jake reached out his webbed hand to touch Emily's back. He paused just a moment. What if this wasn't Emily?

Jake gulped. Any other girl but Emily would scream, and all the kids on the bleachers would see him. Would they still think he was wearing a costume? Or would they know the truth: that Jake really was a swamp monster?

It was a chance he had to take. He tapped the dark-haired girl on the shoulder. Emily turned around, and Jake breathed a sigh of relief. Without a word, Jake pointed to a big bush.

Jake crawled over to the bush, and in just a few minutes Emily met him there.

"What are you doing here?" Emily whispered. "Some of the kids were ready to call animal control yesterday. Andrew brought a net to school today. He wants to catch you and prove you're a swamp monster."

"I had to warn you," Jake said. "You have to cancel graduation practice."

Emily smiled. "That's impossible. They

built this new stage and bleachers just for this year's graduation. Besides, you're supposed to speak at the ceremony. It is a big honor to be asked."

Jake shook his pointy green head. "What would I talk about, anyway?"

"Talk about how it feels to be a hero and save your friends," Emily told him. She gave Jake a big smile, and Jake's green skin turned red in embarrassment.

"No, you don't understand," Jake said. "We have to find a way to cancel graduation, or The Big One will have a feeding frenzy. He promised to come back and eat you."

Emily's eyes popped wide open. She thought a minute before she said, "I have an idea."

7

Closed

That afternoon, Emily taped a big poster to the back of the bleachers. In big red letters, it read: DANGEROUS! SWAMP CLOSED DUE TO POLLUTION.

"What's pollution?" Jake asked.

"That's empty bottles and old cans," Emily told him.

"What's wrong with that?" Jake said. "Swamp monsters find them all the time and use them. We are constantly amazed at the good stuff humans throw away."

Emily frowned. "It messes up the environment," she explained. "The chemicals that poison animals are the worst kind of

DANGEROUS!
SWAMP CLOSED
DUE TO POLLUTION

pollution. Some chemicals could kill everything in the swamp."

Jake stared at Emily. Could she be telling the truth? What kind of horrible people would actually do something like that?

"We can't let them put chemicals in the swamp!" Jake shouted. Then he quickly looked behind him to make sure no one else was around. Luckily, the swamp area was deserted, except for a lone duck sunning itself by the shore.

"Don't worry," Emily told Jake. "The swamp isn't really polluted. Well, not too much, anyway. We're just pretending that it is so they will cancel graduation."

Jake nodded. That made sense. No one would want to be around that evil stuff called pollution. "I just hope it works," he said.

Jake waded back in the water, and Emily

headed home to do her homework. Just in case, Jake kept watch on the shoreline.

A few minutes after Emily left, Principal Pellman walked into the clearing where the stage and bleachers stood. Her arms were full of graduation decorations. She stopped dead in her tracks when she saw Emily's sign.

Jake smiled from his hiding place behind a clump of weeds. Emily's idea had worked. Principal Pellman wouldn't want the students from her school to be around pollution.

But Principal Pellman didn't give up. She pulled a little black box from her pocket and punched it with her finger. Then she talked into it. She jammed the black box back into her pocket and started putting up decorations around the stage. She hung a blue banner in front. It spelled out: CONGRATULATIONS.

Didn't the principal know about pollution? Jake wondered. *Why didn't she leave?* He soon got an answer. Three men in uniforms showed up with big suitcases. They talked to Principal Pellman, snapped open their cases, and put on big rubber gloves. The men took glass bottles out of the big cases and scooped up swamp water. Jake watched

them add different colored liquids to the bottles. In just a few minutes, the men talked to Principal Pellman. Then the men packed up and left. With a smile, Principal Pellman ripped down Emily's sign. She finished decorating the stage, and then she left, too.

The swamp was very quiet, except for the lapping of water on the shore. Jake shook his head. It looked like the graduation was still on.

Suddenly, there was a squawk. Jake looked over to where the sleeping duck had been. Feathers were flying as The Big One snapped its jaws shut. Without another sound, the large alligator slid back into the water.

Jake gulped. He had to think of a way to stop graduation. If Nancy had heard The Big One right, he would stop at nothing to eat Emily and her friends.

8

Stage

Jake felt something move in the swamp behind him. It grabbed him by the shoulder. "Awwww!" he screamed. The Big One had him!

"Relax," said Nancy. "It's just me."

Jake felt his face turn red. He didn't want his sister to think he was a baby. "I just saw The Big One eat a duck," Jake explained.

"Is that gator still here?" Nancy asked with a worried look on her green face.

"No, I think he left," Jake said, and he saw his sister relax.

"You have to help me think of a way to stop graduation."

"What is graduation, anyway?" Nancy asked.

Jake shrugged and pointed toward the wooden platform on the shore. "It has something to do with that stage."

Nancy parted the weeds to stare at the bleachers and stage. "Why don't you just get rid of the stage, then?" she asked.

Jake looked at his little sister and smiled. "Nancy, you're a genius!"

"I know," she said simply. "Come on, I'll help you so we can get home before dinnertime."

Jake and Nancy looked first to make sure no humans were in sight. Then they bravely stepped out of the safety of the swamp. Jake pulled hard on a piece of the stage. The wood popped right off. Luckily, swamp monsters are very strong, and in less than

twenty minutes the stage was no more. A big pile of wood lay in its place.

"I feel bad. We destroyed someone's property," Nancy said. "That's not right."

"We only did it to keep people from being eaten," Jake reminded her.

"You're right," Nancy agreed. "Let's hide this wood and get back into the swamp. My skin is drying out like crazy."

Plop. Plop. Plop. The wood was quickly hidden behind a clump of bushes. *Splash. Splash. Splash.* Nancy and Jake slid back into the swamp. Jake swam toward home with a big grin on his face, showing his orange teeth. Now, they would definitely have to cancel graduation.

9

Seaweed Cereal and Mudshakes

"It's impossible!" Jake screamed to himself.

The stage was together again. A man in a blue shirt picked up some tools, dusted off his hands, and walked away from the rebuilt wooden platform.

Jake swam back home as fast as he could. His dad was just putting Jake's breakfast on the big rock they used as a table.

"Good morning Jake," his father said cheerfully. "We've got seaweed cereal with mudshakes. I hope you're hungry."

Eating was the last thing Jake had on his

mind, but he managed a smile and said, "Thanks, Dad." Swamp monsters didn't waste food.

Jake sat down beside Nancy to eat. "Mom went snake hunting," Nancy explained. "And Dad just finished eating. You're late."

Jake nodded, but didn't explain why he was late. He took a bite of cereal, but it stuck in his throat. Even with a swig of mudshake, he had trouble swallowing his favorite breakfast.

Finally, his dad left the kitchen, and Jake grabbed Nancy's arm. "Something terrible happened," Jake told his sister.

"The Big One ate Emily?" Nancy said with her eyes wide.

"No!" Jake said in horror. "At least, not yet. But someone put the stage back together early this morning."

"You're kidding," Nancy said, wiping mudshake off her lip.

"I wish I was," Jake said sadly. "What am I going to do?"

"Maybe there's nothing you *can* do," Nancy told him. "Mom and Dad warned you about going on dry land again. They won't help you. And I have to help Aunt Freda strip mangrove bark for medicine."

"Then I'll ask Cousin Dominick," Jake said. "I'll ask everyone I can find."

Jake quickly rinsed out his cereal bowl and mudshake cup before hurrying over to his Cousin Dominick's house.

"Are you crazy?" Dominick told him from underneath his blanket of braided willow leaves. "The Big One can kill a swamp monster with one swipe of his tail."

"But if we all fight The Big One together, he won't stand a chance," Jake told his sleepy cousin.

"No!" Dominick yelled before falling back to sleep.

Jake raced all over the swamp monster community. No one listened to him. No one wanted to help webless creatures.

Jake gulped and headed for the stage. He'd have to save Emily all by himself.

10

Hero

Jake stuck his head out of the swamp. The bleachers were already filled with people for graduation. Jake didn't see Emily anywhere. Luckily, he didn't see The Big One, either.

If that huge gator showed up, Jake needed to be close by to help, so he edged up to the shore and hid in a big clump of swamp grass. Jake shivered when he realized that this was just the place where an alligator would love to hide.

Jake kept his eyes glued on the swamp, looking for any movement. That's why he didn't see Principal Pellman walking up behind him. “There you are,” she said, grabbing him by the shoulder. “We’re about to get started. I’m glad I found you.”

Principal Pellman dragged Jake behind the stage, not giving him a chance to say a word. “For goodness’ sake, take off that costume,” she told him. “You’re speaking first.”

Jake gulped. How could he talk at graduation? He had no idea what to say. Principal Pellman walked on stage to introduce him, and Jake got ready to run back to the swamp.

“Here,” whispered a voice behind a nearby bush. It was Emily! She must have been watching for him, like he was watching for The Big One. Emily held out a carrot, and Jake grabbed it. He slipped behind another bush and quickly bit into the carrot.

The next thing he knew, Jake's head hurt, and the trees looked fuzzy. His stomach didn't feel very good, either. Jake looked at his hands. Pale skinny fingers replaced his green webs. He was no longer a swamp monster. The carrot had turned him human!

This wasn't the first time carrots had worked their magic on Jake. He'd been a human before. The first time was when he'd sampled some carrots someone had thrown in the swamp trash can. That's when he'd become friends with Emily. He had even gone to her school. Still, Jake didn't think he'd ever get used to not having gills. It just wasn't normal. Luckily, Jake had on some swim trunks he'd found on the shore. Webless creatures had strange ideas about wearing clothes, whereas swamp monsters didn't need them.

With blurry eyes, Jake saw Principal Pellman motioning to him and saying, "Jake, tell us about being a hero." She stood off to the side of the stage to make room for Jake.

Jake stumbled onto the stage and up to the wooden podium. Principal Pellman shook her head at Jake's swimming trunks. Jake kept his eyes on the water, checking for The Big One. The microphone squeaked when Jake spoke into it. "Um, I guess being a hero is about not caring what others think, but doing what's right."

He paused and was surprised at all the people staring at him. Hundreds of webless creatures of all sizes and shapes looked at him from the bleachers. "Doing the right thing means that sometimes you have to be alone — and it's scary being alone," Jake said slowly. Jake was scared facing all those people. He knew he might have to face The Big One alone, too.

"Do you have any words of advice for our graduating sixth-graders?" Principal Pellman asked Jake, trying to get him to talk longer.

Jake nodded. "Be kind. Study hard, and always, and I do mean always, watch out for snakes and alligators — especially alligators."

Principal Pellman frowned and took the microphone away from Jake. "Thank you Jake. That was, um . . . good advice indeed. Now, let's proceed with handing out the diplomas."

Jake got off the stage as quickly as he could. While everyone was watching the sixth-graders get their diplomas, Jake saw The Big One coming through the swamp.

11

The Real Heroes

Jake gulped. What should he do? No one else saw the ripples in the water and the dark shadow made by The Big One.

How Jake wished he hadn't eaten a carrot. He wondered how long it would be before he turned back into a swamp monster. He was pretty sure it wouldn't be fast enough. The simple fact was that humans just weren't as strong as swamp monsters. Jake didn't stand a chance fighting a huge alligator as a skinny kid.

The Big One made a beeline through the water toward the bleachers, which weren't far from the shore. Jake knew Emily was sitting in there somewhere. The Big One probably knew it, too.

Jake opened his mouth, ready to scream for everyone to run. If they ran now, maybe they could escape in time.

"Hey!" Jake screamed from the side of the stage.

Everyone on the stage stopped. A big, red-haired kid with freckles dropped his rolled-up diploma, and Principal Pellman stopped smiling. "Jake," she said into the microphone. "Is everything okay?"

"There's . . . there's . . . ," Jake started to say. But then he saw something quite amazing. Two swamp monsters stepped in front of The Big One. They were Aunt Freda and his sister Nancy. In just a second, two more popped up out of the swamp beside them—his mom and dad! His dad held his trusty cooking pot firmly in his

webbed hand. Nancy must have gotten their family to help. She was the best sister ever.

Tears filled Jake's eyes as two more swamp monsters popped up—Dominick and a kid from Jake's swamp school. Jake couldn't believe it as more monsters stood up out of the water between The Big One and the shore. It looked like every swamp monster Jake knew had showed up.

"Jake, do you have something else you wanted to say?" Principal Pellman said impatiently.

Jake turned red and slowly walked onstage. He was glad all eyes were on him and not on the water. He didn't want to think about what would happen if all of these webless creatures saw a swamp full of monsters.

"Yes," Jake said. "I forgot to mention something."

"Well, what is it?" Princpal Pelllman asked.

Jake saw The Big One lift its snout and snap a few times before turning around and silently sliding back into the water. The Big One swam back to the darkest part of the swamp. He knew he was outnumbered. He had given up before anyone got hurt.

Jake waved at the audience, but he was really waving at his family and friends. They had helped the webless creatures after all. Jake's human heart felt like it would pop out of his chest.

"I just wanted to say that I'm not the only hero around here," he said into the microphone. "My family and friends are the best. They are true heroes — each and every one."

With that, Jake's eyes searched the audience. His gaze met Emily's, and she

gave him a wink. Jake walked off the stage feeling weak with excitement. Just as he passed behind a clump of swamp grass, he felt his gills and webs grow back. He slipped into the swamp, knowing that he and his family and friends had saved the day.